# The Little Girl Who Loves to Doodle

## Alice Bey-Pugh

She likes to draw...

...but she loves to doodle.

She is an artist as you can see.

She even doodles on Blue…
The next door neighbor's dog.

Her dad calls it creative...
and her mom calls
it a masterpiece.

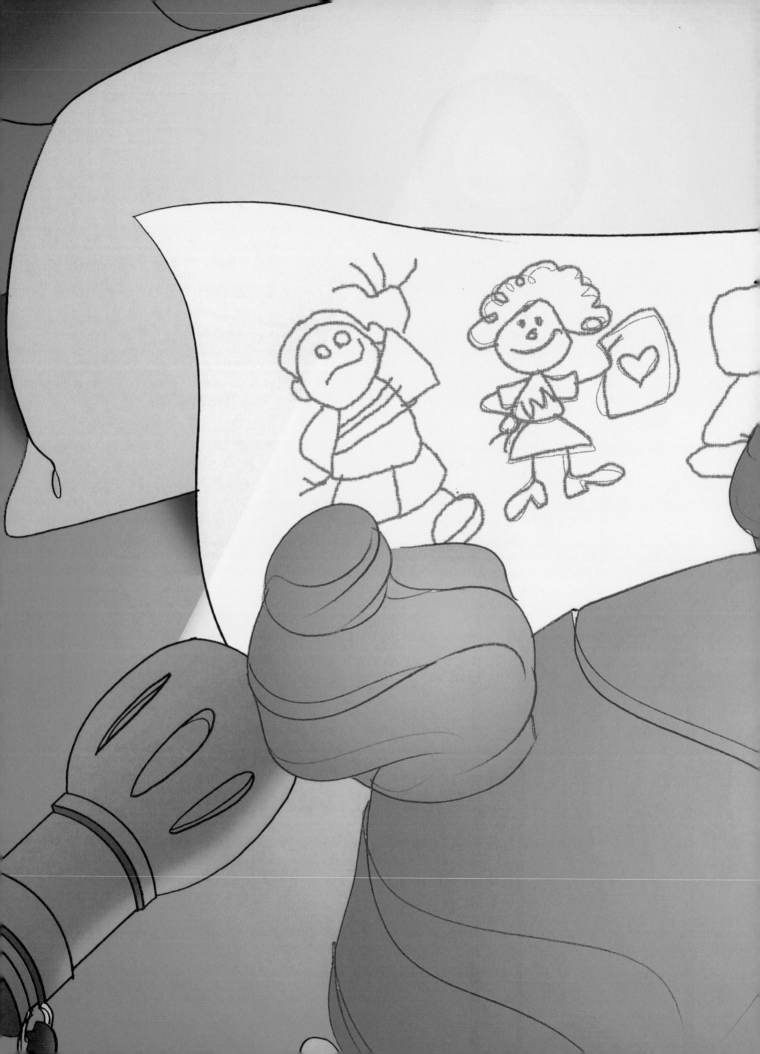

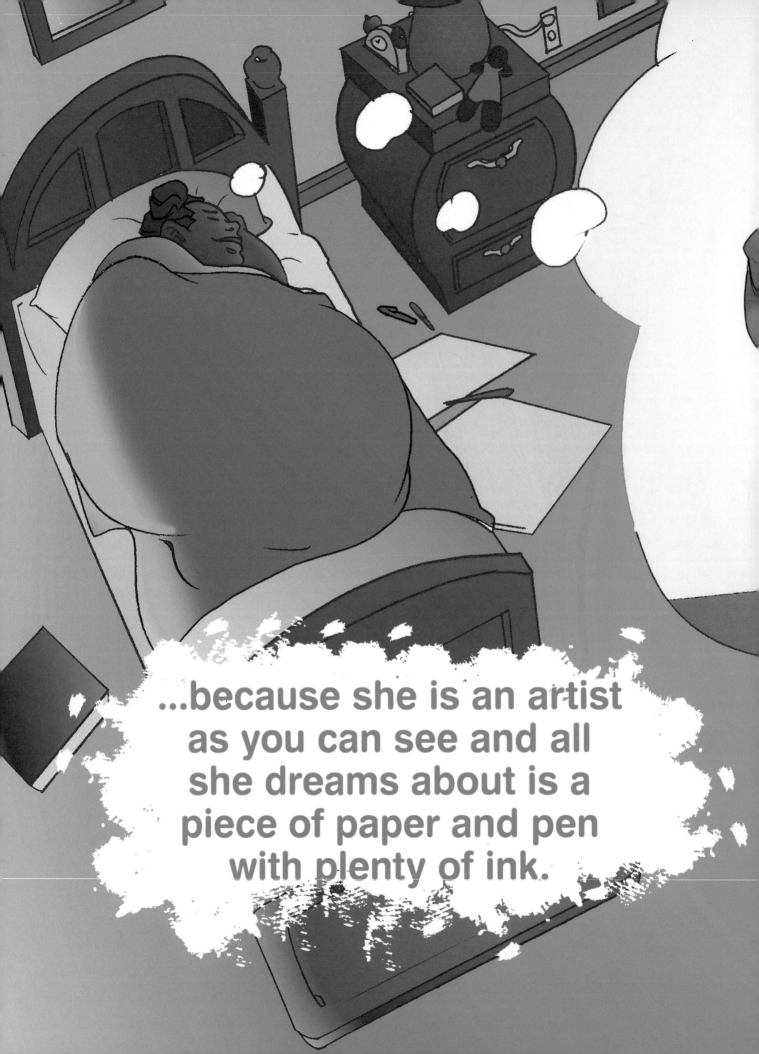

AuthorHouse™
1663 Liberty Drive
Bloomington, IN 47403
www.authorhouse.com
Phone: 833-262-8899

Because of the dynamic nature of the Internet, any web addresses or links contained in this book may have changed
since publication and may no longer be valid. The views expressed in this work are solely those of the author and do not
necessarily reflect the views of the publisher, and the publisher hereby disclaims any responsibility for them.

Any people depicted in stock imagery provided by Getty Images are models,
and such images are being used for illustrative purposes only.
Certain stock imagery © Getty Images.

This book is printed on acid-free paper.

ISBN: 978-1-5246-0798-2 (sc)
ISBN: 978-1-5246-0799-9 (e)

Library of Congress Control Number: 2016907632

Print information available on the last page.

Published by AuthorHouse  10/20/2023

authorHOUSE®

Printed in the United States
by Baker & Taylor Publisher Services